Parents and Caregivers,

Stone Arch Readers are designed to provide enjoyable reading experiences, as well as opportunities to develop vocabulary, literacy skills, and comprehension. Here are a few ways to support your beginning reader:

- Talk with your child about the ideas addressed in the story.

- Discuss each illustration, mentioning the characters, where they are, and what they are doing.

- Read with expression, pointing to each word. You may want to read the whole story through and then revisit parts of the story to ensure that the meanings of words or phrases are understood.

- Talk about why the character did what he or she did and what your child would do in that situation.

- Help your child connect with characters and events in the story.

Remember, reading with your child should be fun, not forced. Each moment spent reading with your child is a priceless investment in his or her literacy life.

Gail Saunders-Smith, Ph.D.

illustrated by
Andy Rowland

STONE ARCH READERS

are published by Stone Arch Books,
a Capstone Imprint
151 Good Counsel Drive
P.O. Box 669
Mankato, Minnesota 56002
www.capstonepub.com

Library of Congress Cataloging-in-Publication data is available on the Library of Congress website.
ISBN: 978-1-4342-2509-2 (library binding)
ISBN: 978-1-4342-3050-8 (paperback)

Summary: Gary needs a new pair of shoes and has a lot of choices.

Reading Consultants:
Gail Saunders-Smith, Ph.D.
Melinda Melton Crow, M.Ed.
Laurie K. Holland, Media Specialist

Art Director/Designer: Kay Fraser
Production Specialist: Michelle Biedscheid

Printed in the United States of America in Stevens Point, Wisconsin.
092010   005934WZS11

Little Lizard's
NEW
SHOES

by Melinda Melton Crow

STONE ARCH BOOKS
a capstone imprint

This is Dad Lizard.
This is Mom Lizard.
This is Gary Lizard.

"Oh no!" said Gary.
"Look at my shoes!"

"You need some new shoes,"
said Mom.

"Oh boy!" said Gary.

The family goes to the
shoe store.

Gary looks at the
blue shoes.

Gary looks at the
orange shoes.

Gary looks at the green shoes.

19

"Which ones do you like?"
said Dad.

"I like the orange shoes,"
said Gary.

"I can run fast," said Gary.

"I can jump high," said Gary.

Gary gets the orange shoes.

Gary runs and jumps
all the way home.

STORY WORDS

shoes   store   high

family   orange   home

Total Word Count: 95

Little Lizard's BOOKSTORE

NEW TITLES